Have you ever
lost a baby tooth,
placed it under your
pillow and found a coin
left by the Tooth Fairy?
In many countries around
the world, there is no such
thing as the Tooth Fairy.
Instead there is ...

For my not-so-little girls, Emily and Allison,
and of course, for Tara — S.H.

Pour ma petite souris, Félix — J.N.

Text © 2012 Susan Hood
Illustrations © 2012 Janice Nadeau

Kids Can Press acknowledges the financial support of the Government of
Ontario, through the Ontario Media Development Corporation's Ontario
Book Initiative; the Ontario Arts Council; the Canada Council for the Arts;
and the Government of Canada, through the BPIDP, for our publishing activity.

Published in Canada by
Kids Can Press Ltd.
25 Dockside Drive
Toronto, ON M5A 0B5

Published in the U.S. by
Kids Can Press Ltd.
2250 Military Road
Tonawanda, NY 14150

www.kidscanpress.com

The artwork in this book was rendered in pencil and watercolor.
The text is set in Adobe Bernhard Modern.

Edited by Tara Walker
Designed by Karen Powers

This book is smyth sewn casebound.
Manufactured in Tseung Kwan O, NT Hong Kong, China,
in 3/2012 by Paramount Printing Co. Ltd.

CM 12 0 9 8 7 6 5 4 3 2 1

Library and Archives Canada Cataloguing in Publication

Hood, Susan
    The tooth mouse / written by Susan Hood ; illustrated by Janice Nadeau.

ISBN 978-1-55453-565-1

I. Nadeau, Janice II. Title.

PZ7.H758Too 2012   j813'.54   C2011-907952-6

Kids Can Press is a *Corus*™ Entertainment company

The Tooth Mouse

WRITTEN BY
Susan Hood

ILLUSTRATED BY
Janice Nadeau

Kids Can Press

Once long ago, atop an ancient cathedral in France,
there lived a small mouse who would NOT go to bed.

"Shush, *chérie*," said the roosting dove. "It's time to sleep."

"But I'm not sleepy," said Sophie. "I want to play Tooth Mouse.
Cranky old cats can't catch me. Watch this!" And Sophie executed
a perfect *pas de chat*.

Then Sophie stopped. She heard a noise.

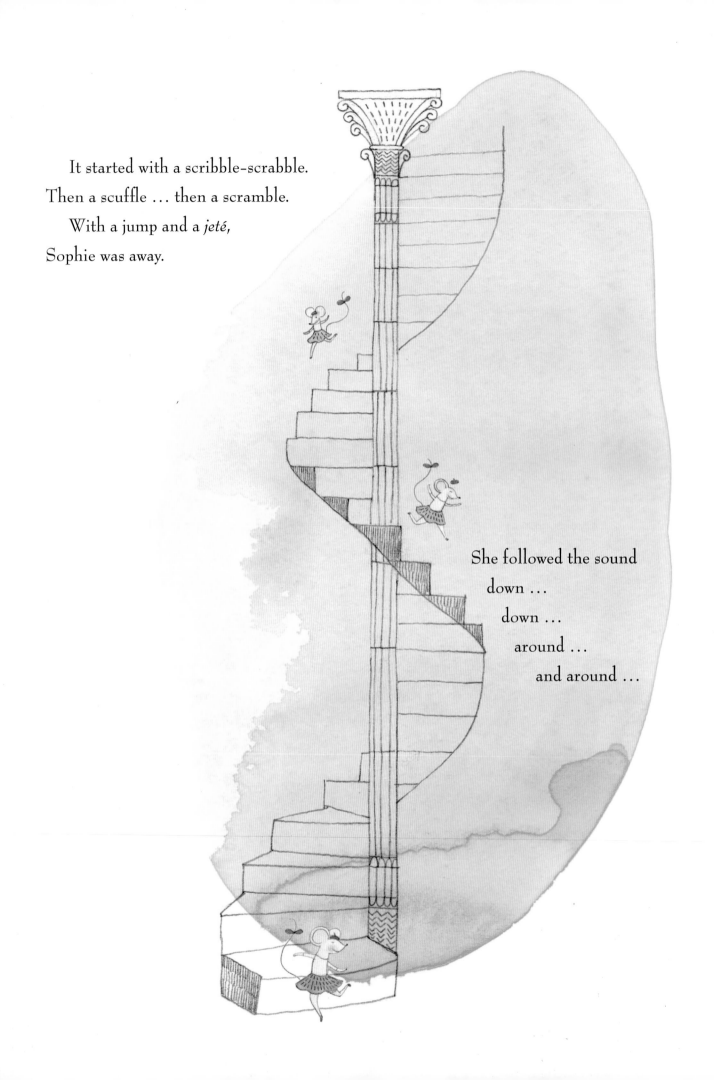

It started with a scribble-scrabble.
Then a scuffle … then a scramble.
With a jump and a *jeté*,
Sophie was away.

She followed the sound
down …
down …
around …
and around …

… until she found herself in the great hall of the cathedral, where a crowd of mice had assembled.

A hush fell over the room. Sophie stood on her tiptoes to see a stern but elegant old mouse appear from the shadows in a shower of moonlight.

Sophie gasped. "It's the Tooth Mouse! *La Petite Souris!*"

"Bon soir," cried the Tooth Mouse. "My friends, as you know, I have served faithfully as the Tooth Mouse for many years — dodging cats, collecting coins and delivering the money to children in exchange for their baby teeth. But I am not as spry as I used to be … I have decided it is time to name my successor!"

"AHHHH!" said the crowd.

"SILENCE!" said the Tooth Mouse. She paused to eye the mice over her spectacles. "All those who wish to be chosen will be given three tasks. You must prove that you are brave, honest and, above all, wise!"

"C'est moi!" thought Sophie. "Choose me! Choose me!"

"For your first task," said the Tooth Mouse, "bring me the whisker of a cat!"

Many mice attempted the first task. Did they all succeed? *Mais non!*

Most were happy to escape with their lives.

Only five returned with the required whisker.

"*Très bien!*" said the Tooth Mouse, eyeing Sophie, the smallest contender, with interest.

"Her whisker doesn't count," complained one mouse. "She's too little to be the Tooth Mouse."

"We shall see, we shall see," said the Tooth Mouse. "Now, you five may be brave. But are you honest? For your second task, bring me a silver coin. Beware! Thievery will not be permitted! I will be watching."

The five mice set about the second task.
Did they all succeed? *Mais non!*

Only three obtained a silver coin by honest means.

They presented the coins to the Tooth Mouse.
"Félicitations!" she said with a hint of a smile.
"You three are brave *and* honest. Now for your third
and most difficult task. Follow me."

The Tooth Mouse led Sophie and the others down dark
corridors into the deep recesses of the cathedral.

She withdrew a key from her cloak and
unlocked a tiny door that opened into
a massive room.

She led the way into the chamber and gestured
to the charts that lined the walls. *"Voilà!* Here are the names
and addresses of the thousands of children who are expected
to lose a tooth in the next three days," she explained.

"What will I do with all those baby teeth? You have until
sunrise tomorrow to present me with a plan."

"Thousands of baby teeth?
Mais non! It is *impossible!*" thought
Sophie, her tail dragging as she
trudged home.

Back atop the cathedral, Sophie slumped against a kindly mother dove. She whispered, "I tried so hard. Now I'll never be the Tooth Mouse."

"Go to sleep, *chérie*," cooed the dove. "Sometimes the wisest answer is the simplest one. I'm sure something will come to you."

That night, Sophie DID go to bed, but she dreamed of teeth.
Shiny teeth, tiny teeth. Munching teeth, crunching teeth.
Chewing, chattering, gnawing, guffawing teeth!
What would she do with thousands
of baby teeth?

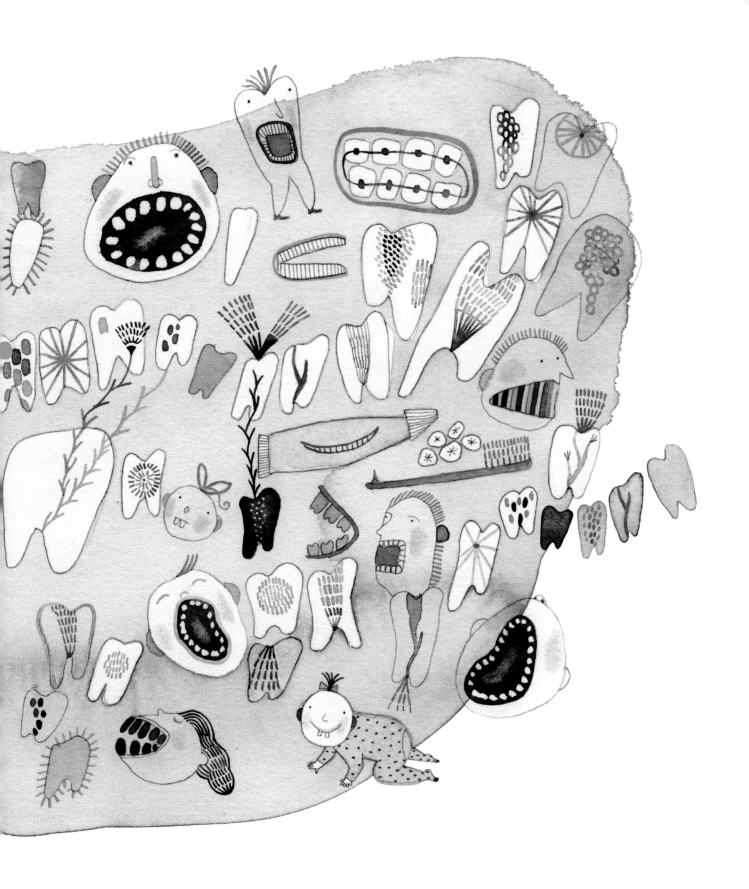

When the little mouse awoke, she sat up and smiled.
Ah! *Mais oui!* Of course!

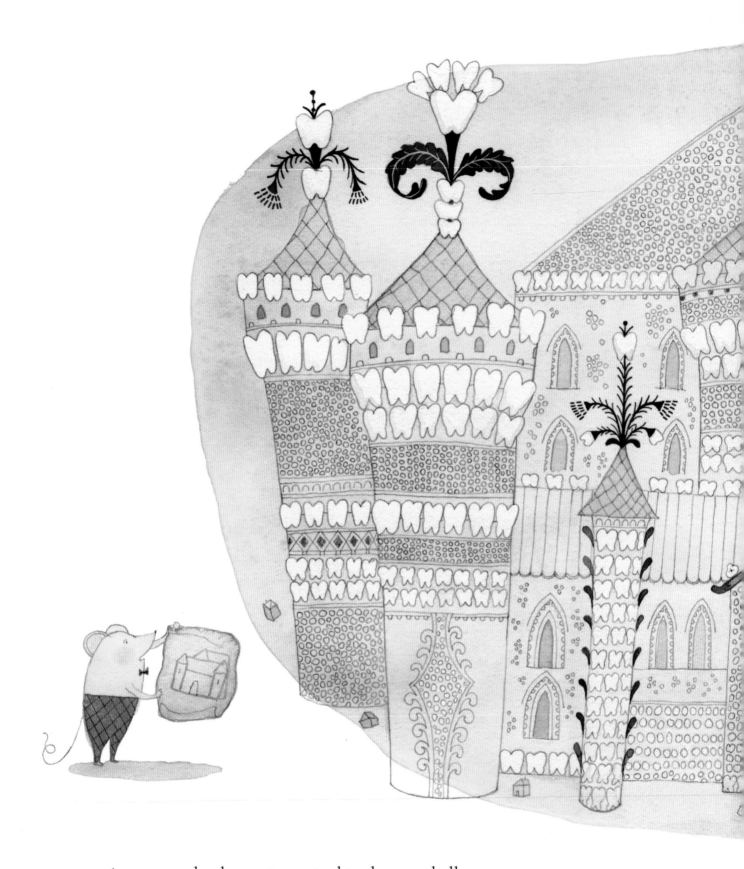

At sunrise, the three mice arrived in the great hall to
present their plans to the Tooth Mouse and the crowd assembled there.
"We could build a castle," said the first mouse, unveiling his idea with a flourish.
"AHHHH!" said the crowd.

"Mais non!" said the Tooth Mouse. "With all the baby teeth,
this castle would cover the kingdom."

The second mouse stepped forward with her
proposal. "We could roll them into the sea," she said.
"AHHHH!" said the crowd.

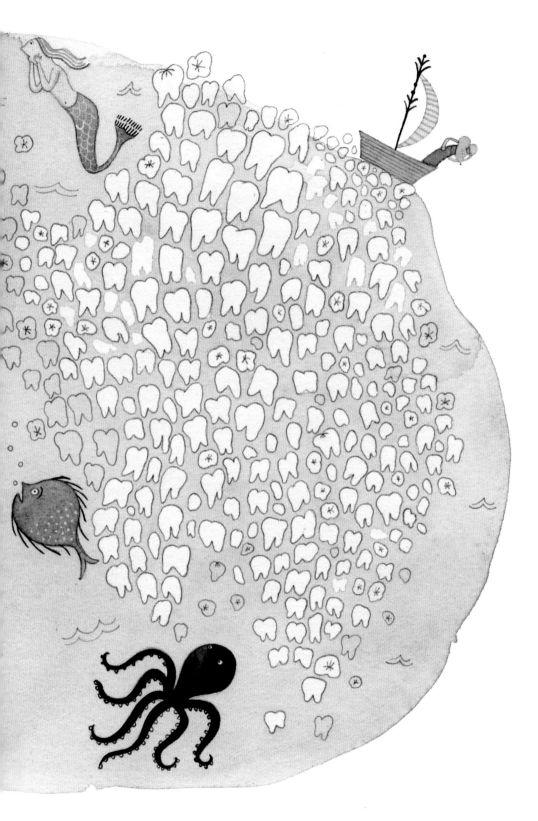

"Mais non!" sniffed the Tooth Mouse.

"With all the baby teeth, we would fill up the sea!"

At last it was Sophie's turn. Her tail twitched as
she unrolled her plan and gave it to the Tooth Mouse.
The Tooth Mouse said nothing as she studied
Sophie's proposal.

Then the aged face broke into a wide smile.
"Ahhhh," she said. *"Mais oui! So simple, so wise."*
She turned to face the crowd. "We have found a
winner. I present to you the NEW Tooth Mouse!"

Sophie, the small mouse who would NOT go to bed, spent the
rest of her nights as the Tooth Mouse, *La Petite Souris*, showing
bravery, honesty and wisdom. She dodged cats, collected coins and
delivered the money to children in exchange for their baby teeth.

And what did she do with all those baby teeth?

She gave them to babies, of course!

La fin.